THE COURT OF ETERNAL AFFAIRS

CASE NO. 1

THE SPIRIT OF TRUTH VS. SATAN

WHY YOU WERE NOT BAPTIZED IN JESUS' NAME

AND WHY YOU Should Be

JIM PICKERING

PUBLISHED BY
OUR WRITTEN LIVES OF HOPE, LLC

Our Written Lives of Hope provides publishing services for authors in various educational, religious, and human service organizations. For information, visit www.OurWrittenLives.com.

Cover & Interior Design by Our Written Lives

Library of Congress Cataloging-in-Publication Data
Pickering, Jim 1945
Why You Were Not Baptized in Jesus Name

Library of Congress Control Number: 2016901394
ISBN: 978-1-942923-11-4 (paperback)

Why You Were Not Baptized in Jesus Name

"I have known Jim Pickering for 35 years. He is a true Christian. If you have ever wondered about baptism in Jesus Name you need to read this book. Here is a new look at an old subject; a must read for every Christian!"

REV. G.R. (BOBBY) EDWARDS, BISHOP, EASTGATE UPC

"An often misunderstood subject comes to life in story form in this book, capturing the attention while educating the mind and soul. The subject of baptism is often misunderstood and Jim Pickering boldly confronts the subject, bringing clarity to why Jesus Name baptism is necessary to salvation. I encourage you to open the pages, be drawn into the story and discover that you must be baptized in Jesus Name!"

REV. AND MRS. MATTHEW TUTTLE, EASTGATE UPC

DEDICATION

Thanks to God.

You deserve the glory. Thank You for the inspiration and burden You gave me to write and publish.

Thanks to my wonderful and supportive wife, Jewel.

You were and are what keeps me together. I love you. Thank you for your patience through every second guess.

Thanks to my family & Friends.

Thanks to my son Jody for each and every invigorating conversation.

Thanks to my son Jonathan for your support, and for every book you have shared or recommended to me.

Hats off to Julia, Joyce, Roy, Gloria, Kathy, Dr. Jamie, and Dr. "Doc" Burke for reading and re-reading and giving honest feedback.

Kudos to Raymond and the Hill clan for taking precious time while on family vacation to review this book.

Special honor extended to:

Rev. Matthew and Michelle Tuttle, my Pastors
Rev. G.R. Edwards, my Bishop

I would be remiss without hearty thanks to Bishop Isaac Ogbeta. Thank you for reading, encouraging and commissioning.

And how can I thank such a magnificent publisher, Rachael K. Hartman. There would be no book without you. You are a writer's gift, and a blessing to God's kingdom.

CONTENTS

INTRODUCTION
AN ETERNAL CASE

I REMEMBER TIMES as a child when I sat listening to sermons and teachings on the subject of baptism. In the 1950's, my pastor, R.D. Gibson, would ask his daughter and son-in-law, Vesta and Gerald Mangun, to speak to our church when they were visiting. Sister Vesta would talk about the work of God's Power in our lives, and the importance of Biblically correct baptism. Over the course of many years, I pondered the variations in baptismal practices and traditions among Christian churches. I continued studying baptism through the years and learned a lot about the history of religious traditions, political influences on organized religion and the variability of Christian practices—such as baptismal mode. I taught on the subject in Sunday school and made baptism the focus of discussion during many Bible study sessions.

Years into my studies, the Lord began calling me to write a book on the subject of baptism. The book, which you now hold in your hand, was not to be a textbook or in-depth look at history. Instead, it would take on a more creative approach. I began to imagine a courtroom where the important cases of eternity are weighed in the balances. That courtroom is called the Court of Eternal Affairs. This book encapsulates one case in particular: The Court of Eternal Affairs versus Satan in the case of *Why You Were Not Baptized in Jesus Name*. The devil goes on trial for perverting the baptismal message.

In my imaginings, I shift from my reality as a curious reader scouring history, into the role of a Prosecuting

Lawyer. I begin to take my time diligently pondering the infamous, though often ignored, crimes against eternity. My approach involves outlining my thought process as I gather evidence of the crime, build my case and call witnesses. Although Satan is on trial here, I will not call him as a witness. As the father of lies (John 8:44) and the deceiver of the whole world (Revelation 12:9), I cannot trust Satan to testify.

In the imaginary courtroom, I have access to witnesses from every century. I can call witnesses from throughout time, the Bible, and political figures seemingly unrelated to Christianity. I can cross-examine historic figures who were key players when it came to the changes in question. Truth will reveal itself through the testimonies, and the jury will decide the verdict.

Truth. That's all that matters, not religious tradition or "the way we've always done it." The Spirit of Truth presides over the Court of Eternal Affairs. He is the ultimate Judge. He leads and guides us to all Truth, and He presides over this book and my journey preparing to enter the Court of Eternal Affairs. It's the weight of the knowledge of eternity that leads me forward in my search for Truth.

Baptism matters. Join me as we begin a journey to uncover the Truth about religious baptismal traditions, and what the Bible has to say about the importance of baptism on eternal salvation. In particular, as you search out your own soul's salvation (Philippians 2:12), the case of *Why You Were Not Baptized in Jesus Name* will serve as a launch pad for your own Biblical and historic quest for Truth. The fact that you are reading this book validates my inspiration to write it. I believe there are many people with honest hearts, like you, who want to think independently about religion and spirituality. You want to know the truth about eternal salvation and what the Bible says is required to make it to Heaven.

In the following chapters, I contemplate the history of baptism, the importance of obedience to God's plan, and the nature of the enemy of our souls and his track record for luring humanity to destruction. I also contemplate the power of the blood of Jesus, and the infallible Truth of the Word of God. After that, it will be time to present the evidence and call on witnesses in one of the most important hearings at the Court of Eternal Affairs—The Spirit of Truth versus Satan, in the case of *Why You Were Not Baptized in Jesus Name.*

CHAPTER 1

ONE CHANCE

A HEAVY WARMTH filled the atmosphere. In the firmament, the area above the horizon, there was something different, out of the ordinary. Brooding, billowing, smoky structures, eerie and foreboding, hovered in the sky. A strange, deep, dark sound caused the air and ground to vibrate. In an instant, a light brighter than anything in the world's memory pierced the distant ground, and a sudden explosion sounded off like a cannon. An intriguing fresh smell filled the air. It's a smell no one experienced before. And then, water drained like tears from Heaven's heaving soul. It was raining for the very first time.

They say there is a first time for everything. And the first rain was definitely of Biblical proportions. In the Genesis 7 account, God, in His disappointment, dealt with the errant mankind He created centuries prior. Now, mind you, God didn't make man as an errant creature; outside help influenced the mutation of humanity from innocent to sinful. But, we will talk about that later. For now, we need to discuss Noah.

Noah, his family, and a literal zoo were shut up tight inside an odd piece of craftsmanship. Some one hundred and twenty years prior to all this stormy weather, Noah had a conversation with God Himself. God, full of justice, was angry about mankind's violence. It was time to purge the earth. Almighty God was the very first marine engineer, and Noah became the founder of a giant shipyard.

There was a plan, a specific plan. There was a special list of materials, and explicit instructions. Obedience to God's plan and instruction led Noah to embrace a most unusual project, and his faith moved him to be (yes, you guessed it) faithful to complete the job. The world depended on Noah's faithfulness, but, sadly, most chose to listen to opinions against Noah. "Who's he kidding?" They asked. "He must be crazy! Don't pay him any mind!"

The then known world had 120 years to hear about Noah and his "project salvation." He followed God's plan and invited everyone to follow it with him. He excluded no one. In a nutshell, the ark was a foreshadowing picture of today's Church.

The plan was specific. There is also a specific plan for today. And those plans are still open for review, but not for revision. The work on today's ark of safety, the Church, is still in progress. Way back then, to be saved from destruction, folks living in the antediluvian world had to get on board the ark before the door shut. They had one hundred and twenty years to get it right. Many chose to ignore the plan of salvation and forgo entering the ark with Noah. For you and me, history doesn't have to repeat itself. The door for our salvation is still open, at least for now.

We only get one chance. There was one ark, and it had one door. There is only one flag at the end of one race; there is only one finish line. We each have one life, and one eternal choice to make. Will we obey the detailed plan of God and find salvation? Or will we choose the flood of destruction?

Bible believers understand the concept of Heaven and Hell. Heaven is the ultimate destination. Depicted as an eternal life of beauty, peace, health, joy and happiness,

Heaven is our intended home. It is the only eternal home our Lord and Savior prepares for us. If you have ever experienced heartfelt worship, the ecstatic spirit-world connection between your soul and God, the One who created our universe, you know something of how the emotional and spiritual atmosphere in Heaven will feel. Heaven is worth going to, regardless of the effort required. We will find souls in Heaven who lived exemplary lives, as well as those who at times did not; the Spirit and Grace of God will have transformed everyone there.

On the other hand, Hell is a place of eternal death, prepared for the devil and his angels. It is a place of continual dying, yet no one will be able to die there though they will wish they could. And, if Hell truly is a bottomless pit, the eternal free-fall will be horrendous. Hell is a lake of fire and brimstone. Hell's excruciating heat and burning sulfur (brimstone) will create an intolerable, acrid, unbreathable environment. People in Hell will be in the company of the worst of the worst of unrepentant sinners, some perhaps even possessed by demons. It is sad to contemplate, but there will be wonderful people in Hell. Honest and moral but unredeemed souls will find themselves in Hell.

For you and me, history doesn't have to repeat itself. The door for our salvation is still open, at least for now.

Our decision on what to believe concerning eternity and salvation is the most important decision we make in our entire lives. In the face of this weighty decision, most of us will take more time deciding what's for lunch today than contemplating where we will live forever. Imagine. Where do you want to live for eternity: Heaven, or Hell? You are the only one who can make your personal choice.

Now that we are thinking about eternity consider this. Many of us have chosen to give reverence to the textbook on the subject of eternal salvation—The Holy Bible—but still rely on second-hand interpretations of the text. Rather than study for ourselves, we allow others to interpret the Bible for us. The Apostle Paul gave good advice in Philippians 2:12, when he said, *"Work out your own salvation with fear and trembling."*

With the glaring fact that eternity is a one-shot proposition with no second chances, there is absolutely no room for error. The Bible is clear: among actions such as belief, trusting in God, repentance, being filled with God's Spirit, and living a life surrendered to God's will, salvation involves baptism. How one is baptized is not to be handled carelessly. Baptism matters, and *how* one is baptized matters as well.

Considering the importance of eternity and salvation, you may find it meaningful to know that people throughout history tampered with some facets of Christian theology to fit their ideology, culture, and time. The changes they made influenced religious practices and became tradition. Often future generations were unaware of any deviation from original Bible doctrine. Many people did not have

Would you allow a pagan priest to tinker with the very Gospel designed to redeem your soul from Hell?

access to a Bible, and when they did they were not encouraged to read it. Thankfully, the Bible and a historic trail of testimony light the way for us to know God's plan of salvation as it was originally presented, exposing what happened along the way.

Ask yourself this: if you had any say in the matter, would you allow a pagan priest to tinker with the very Gospel designed to redeem your soul from Hell? Moreover, would you support the government taking control of your church and manipulating it for national purpose and gain? Would you stand by and allow a lawyer to invent and introduce new words to describe and validate an unbiblical belief that would be incorporated into your church's religious doctrine, a change that could affect your salvation? These are the questions I ask myself as I prepare for The Court of Eternal Affairs.

PART 1

PREPARING FOR COURT

CHAPTER 2

HONEY ROASTED CICADAS

NICKNAMES usually mean something. If a person is nicknamed "Red" we usually only need to look at their hair color, and we understand the origin of their moniker. If folks call you "Smitty," your sir name is undoubtedly Smith, which probably means you or some ancestor worked as a blacksmith. Many last names, such as Cartwright, Shepherd, and Baker, reflect past occupations and avocations.

In the Bible, a man named John had a nickname. Everyone called him "John the Baptist," or, a better translation, "John the baptizer." A baptizer, how odd! John himself was a little odd as well. We could call him peculiar, to say the least. Living in the wild, John was somewhat apart from society. He was a wilderness dweller—one who ate locusts and wild honey, foods considered delicacies in the region today. He wore clothes made of rough camel's hair and a leather girdle.

When John the Baptizer came to town, people noticed. Had you lived in his day, it would have been good for you to take notice of the strange man, different as he was. To hear his message and allow John to baptize you would have been a blessing. The whole concept of baptism was new to the people of John's day, and they probably considered it a fairly bizarre activity—like the man preaching it. Although the life of John the Baptist is not the theme of this book, his occupation, baptism, is.

Culturally, John the Baptist provided a necessary introduction to the baptismal concept. He also brought a new focus to the concept of personal repentance, the sorrowful turning away from wrongdoing and the shift to righteous living—another aspect of the salvation process. In the Old Testament, salvation came through the annual sacrifice. It was a yearly rolling forward of sins accomplished by the bloodshed of an innocent animal. Baptism was not a part of their rituals at that time.

Long before John the Baptist extolled, *"Repent ye: for the kingdom of heaven is at hand"* (Matthew 3:1-2), people took a personal trip to the Temple and sacrificed whatever animal they could afford to rid themselves of their sin for one more year. History tells us that the annual sacrifices stopped some six hundred years prior to John's call to repentance. People abandoned worship at the Temple when enemy forces destroyed it. So, for many years, no sacrifice was offered, and no sins rolled forward. I can only imagine the weight of guilt and shame passed down from generation to generation.

History is invaluable in understanding the present.

John preached the message of repentance with an accompanying water baptism, but there was more to his message! There was a promise: *"There cometh one mightier than I after me, the latchet of whose shoes I am not worthy to stoop down and unloose"* (Mark 1:7).

Who was the "One" John spoke of, and why, all of a sudden, was baptism so important? These are the first questions I encounter as I begin to analyze the court case before me.

John provided the answer of the "One" when he

introduced Jesus. I can almost hear John's voice, *"Behold the Lamb of God, which taketh away the sin of the world"* (John 1:29). Jesus was the ultimate sacrifice for sin. Israel was not the only group of people to reap the great spiritual blessings of Jesus' sacrifice; the redemption plan was for every nation. Jesus was *"the Lamb of God"* and would *"take away the sin of the world."*

Huge as the task may have seemed, redeeming us from sin was Jesus' core mission. With Jesus as the ultimate sacrifice for sin, a yearly sacrifice would no longer be necessary. Until Jesus came, no one associated the security of their soul with the water-based submersion we call baptism. With the birth of the New Testament Church, baptism became a necessary component of salvation. Mark 16:16 says, *"He that believeth and is baptized shall be saved . . ."* Now, repentance, baptism and remission of sin would become central to salvation's plan. And, as I stated in the introduction, if baptism is important, then how it is administered is important as well.

Baptism, repentance, the blood of Jesus—it all ties together. Understanding these concepts guide me as I prepare for court. And yet, I realize, as important as repentance and the blood of Jesus are, the court case is about baptism. The Christian world agrees on the concept of repentance and the redemptive power of the blood of Jesus. From the time John first preached repentance until now, the world welcomes repentance as an avenue to carry away pent up guilt and crushed consciences. Christians everywhere accept Jesus as the sacrifice for sin and acknowledge the saving power of His blood.

Christians accept baptism too. I have never personally

heard of any convert refusing to be baptized (except for an occasional person who has a fear of water). I *have* heard of a diversity of baptismal modes and methods. The differences and places of division within the Christian church are the reasons we are going to court. Satan is all about division, tearing the unity of the church to shreds. It's a crime worth prosecuting, but I still have much research to prepare and many questions to answer.

I encounter the answers to my questions by taking a retrospective look at the Bible of Ancient Israel. History is invaluable in understanding the present. The Apostle Paul encouraged people to study, especially to study the scriptures. In Galatians 3:24, he wrote that the Word of God leads us to Christ. *"Wherefore the law was our schoolmaster to bring us unto Christ, that we might be justified by faith."*

If you are familiar with Bible stories, you will likely recall in the book of Exodus how the Israelites crossed the Red Sea. The miracle of the people walking through the parted waters typifies baptism. Theologians refer to Old Testament happenings which mirror New Testament principles as "types and shadows." The Red Sea crossing is a type or shadow of baptism.

Another notable type or shadow of baptism is the Old Testament story of Naaman the leper. Picture Naaman's outrage as the Prophet Elisha instructed him to proceed to the Jordan River and dip down in it seven times. Naaman thought the Jordan was too muddy, but when he finally humbled himself and obeyed, God restored him to health and cleansed away his leprosy. Here, leprosy is symbolic of sin. Naaman's story is a beautiful picture of how confessed sin is washed away in baptism. Humility and obedience result in the miraculous.

Another rich example of baptismal cleansing found in the Old Testament is the golden laver, which stood in the outer court of the Tabernacle in the wilderness. It was a washing or cleansing water spot where the priests washed their hands from the blood of the animal sacrifices.

In the New Testament, people baptized by immersion—that means dunking the person fully under water—as they called on the name of the Lord. The traditional church practiced baptism by total immersion until somewhere around 240 AD. A new practice came onto the scene at that time, with the baptism of a man named Novatian who procrastinated making his decision for baptism. Sick to the point of death and unable to move from his bed, Novatian allowed zealous believers to pour water on him in order to "baptize" him.

Humility and obedience result in the miraculous.

Within a few decades, Roman Catholic Priests began "baptizing" legions of Roman soldiers as they marched in formation beside various bodies of water. The priests wielded tree branches, dipping them into the adjacent water and slinging water droplets across the ranks of soldiers in a mass baptismal ritual, likely without the soldier's consent or prior repentance. Sometime around the seventh century AD, the Roman Catholic Church introduced another form of baptism: infant baptism by sprinkling.

There are variations of baptismal practices. When, why and how did rituals change? Is there any consistency concerning baptism? What is the bottom line truth? What is the Biblical standard we should look to as we practice baptism in our lives? Thus, my journey of preparation to argue before the Court of Eternal Affairs continues.

CHAPTER 3

SPECIFIC INSTRUCTIONS

THE SMELL OF SPICY FOOD was so thick I could almost cut the scent with my butter knife. My imagination was alive with delight. I was about to enjoy a new cuisine. The food was one of the best experiences of visiting Savannah, Georgia.

As our server approached the table, I could see I was in for a treat. He brought oysters and clams still in the shell. The king crab legs and shrimp cooked to perfection invited me with their warm orange and coral hues. Steam sauntered into the heavens from the top of a bowl piled high with boiled golden corn on the cob and halved red-potatoes. And, of course, there was ample buttery sauce to dunk it all in. The aroma of "Old Bay Seasoning" was delightful. What a combination; it was dynamite for the taste buds!

Relishing in the memories of that magnificent meal, I turn to the Bible to continue my study. I refocus on 1 Kings, Chapter 17. According to the Biblical account, the prophet Elijah spoke a Word from God to King Ahab—there would be a serious drought. Because of a lack of rain in Israel, there would be no feasts such as the one I enjoyed in Savannah. For a time, a squadron of ravens would airlift food to nourish Elijah as he sat beside the water brook Cherith. It was a notable miracle of nature itself; ravens never choose to share food! Even the word "ravenous" derives from the same root word that gives the raven its name. Amazingly, God chose to use these stingy birds to feed the prophet.

Eventually, the brook Cherith dried up, and it was time for Elijah to change venues. Cherith was a place of solitude, except for the daily raven visit. Eventually, Elijah heard the voice of God leading him into the company of others. The Word of the Lord told Elijah to move to Zarephath and directed him specifically to a certain widow who lived there. Elijah would be the catalyst for God's blessings to the widow and her son. As a result of his obedience and attention to God's detailed instruction, other people would come to experience the miraculous provision of God's favor and witness His power.

God is a God of specifics, and He gives detailed instructions.

Upon arriving in Zarephath, Elijah found the woman's "restaurant" closing down. She and her son were gathering wood to build a fire in the oven one last time. There was only enough meal and oil for one last cake of bread. She and her son were going to eat for the last time and then prepare to die of starvation.

Imagine the woman's reaction to Elijah's request: "Make my cake first." There was no "first" and "second." Didn't he hear her? What didn't he understand about "the *last* cake of bread." She didn't mind getting him a drink of water, but the cake was their last ration of food.

But, she thought, if they were going to starve, what difference would it make to prolong it by one day? So she baked him the cake of bread. As the woman and her son sat down to watch the last morsel of food disappear at the hands of a stranger, the prophet made an even more bizarre request. "Bake another cake to satisfy your hunger."

Reluctantly, she furtively gazed into the meal barrel. What was that? She asked herself. There seemed to be a little more meal there. There was about enough for another cake. As they all ate together, the woman wondered how making another cake was possible.

Such a fragile, questioning trust was probably no stronger the next day, when Elijah again instructed her as before, "Make mine first." And, to her surprise, there was still a little meal and oil. Maybe she miscalculated. Could it be her eyesight was going? These thoughts haunted her.

By the third day, I imagine, she began to realize the miracle. She was pretty good at measuring meal. She knew how much was required to bake a cake of bread. She also knew when the oil barely trickled out of the cruise it was all but long gone. Yet each time she went to bake, it was evident there was enough for one more. Amazing!

To bring us to the point I'm making, we need to think about the scientific method for a moment. Simply put, science dictates a precise method for experimentation. We must take meticulous notes as we change only one facet of an experiment at a time. It is in the copious details that we can observe and analyze any effect from the particular change we made.

In a similar way, if a baker wishes to vary a cake recipe he should change only one ingredient or detail at a time to discover the key to his desired end product. The scientific method is effective if sufficient time and resources are available to carry through with the experiment.

Experiments paid off generously for Thomas Edison as he refined the light bulb to a viable, useful stage. Never mind that it took thousands of attempts before he finally succeeded. He kept at it, changing one minor detail after another until he had results that led to success. We applaud him. We appreciate his work. But in Elijah's world there was no time for thousands of experiments. He had to get it right, the *first* time.

Humans must eat to survive. So Elijah had to listen to and obey God's instructions. God is a God of specifics, and He gives detailed instructions. Thankfully, in this case, Elijah already knew about God's attention to detail. He had already experienced similar tight spots. He had already seen other victories through compliance to God's specific instructions. By faith, Elijah had waited for the birds to bring his meals. He knew the Lord's ways were higher than our ways. He trusted the Lord's voice and obeyed.

Elijah, the widow, and her son found nourishment for many days with bread meal that probably never even covered the bottom of the barrel, yet it was enough for each day. Symbolically, the meal and oil are the Word and the Spirit. God provides just enough for our daily bread. We must gather the manna every morning—we can't store it up. We must search the scriptures daily, and nourish our souls with God's provisions and detailed instructions for the day.

According to 1 Corinthians 10:7, *"Now all these things happened unto them for ensamples: and they are written for our admonition . . ."* This passage of Scripture makes reference to happenings in Israel's past. It also points to a successful future for those willing to learn. We can benefit from the stories of Noah and Elijah, and all those who listen to God with a careful ear. We can be encouraged in the fact that God provides a way of escape, a means of survival, in every era or dispensation of time.

I invite you to join me in pondering the prospects of how we live out our quest for salvation. If God is such a specific God (*go to a certain widow in a certain place and tell her a specific thing to do*), and eternity allows for no second chances (*or thousands of second chances, as in the case of Mr. Edison*), then how can we succeed with only one shot at getting it right? The answer is found in the detailed instructions God left for us.

CHAPTER 4

ONE WORD

THE AIR THIS MORNING is crisp, the blue sky cloudless. I am ready to walk my two miles on the track at our community park, named in honor of my late friend Raymond. Birds and squirrels are on active duty today. With the temperature in the low 60s, it feels like the perfect day.

My work schedule has kept me from walking as regularly as I would like to, so today I am interested to see if this near seventy-year-old can still hold the pace. My cardiologist would be interested too, and he would not be pleased to know how often I am absent from regular walking. Using my cell phone as a stopwatch, I start my two miles right on the minute.

My focus is on my stride, my breathing, and how I feel overall. I am not out of breath, I feel no leg aches, and lap after lap I have a general feeling of wellbeing. I enjoy the euphoria that follows. As I finish my last lap it becomes apparent: my time is off. The two miles that usually take 31 minutes to complete, today, take 32. I lost one minute.

Not bad, you say, for a seventy-year-old. I agree. Still something is different. I could blame it on breakfast, last night's rest, or my shoes, but the truth is, I lost a minute. Something changed inside. I am older and losing ground. It is just one little minute, but it *is* a measurable change.

My experience brings to mind Mr. Edison and his light bulb again. For all the good of his innovative research, his bright invention would mean little without electrical current. Edison would not have invented electric light without the development of electrical energy first. A major turning point in many of Edison's discoveries happened years before, with men like James Watt and Robert Fulton. Watt was involved in early prototype steam engine design. Fulton harnessed the power of steam to propel his riverboat and began an industrial revolution. Soon, steam powered assembly lines, textile mills, and power plants producing electricity prompted a wave of discovery that revolutionized our world. We may owe more credit to Fulton than to Edison. Who knows?

There is power in one—one minute, one degree, one word.

When it comes to the converting of combustible material into steam, consider this: the electricity generated in a steam-powered dynamo depends on specific scientific laws. Water converts to steam at sea level at the temperature of 212 degrees Fahrenheit (or 100 degrees Celsius). The volume ratio of water to steam is 1/1700. In other words, in a pressure containment vessel, one gallon of water theoretically becomes over one thousand gallons of steam once the water reaches its boiling point. The volume expansion creates tremendous pressure, which then converts into useful energy.

But enough of scientific formulas. I am not happy with my two miles in 32 minutes, and you would not be happy with your electricity, or lack thereof, at 211 degrees Fahrenheit. Just one degree makes a tremendous difference. Water will not produce steam if it does not reach the boiling point, and without steam Edison couldn't generate electricity. Edison's light bulb would be dark without that one degree. Without that one degree, we wouldn't have mass-produced textiles and the steamship would not head out to sea. It may be small, but one degree makes a big difference—just one degree—just one minute.

There is power in one—one minute, one degree, one word. In the Garden of Eden, there was one word that made a difference. The word was "*not*," and it changed everything.

Every day in the Garden of Eden was perfect. It was a perfect place, inhabited by perfect people, created by a perfect God. It was perfect until one day—the day of one word.

"*Now, the serpent was subtil, more than any other beast of the field,*" according to Geneses 3:1. Satan wanted to muddy the water of perfection. He was not happy with the Garden of Eden and the communion Adam and Eve had with God. He was not happy with his rebellious failure as an archangel. Misery loves company, and he wanted the company of God's perfectly created beings. Satan wanted to see Adam and Eve fail. But how would he proceed? He had a plan, and it revolved around one word.

In all His creating, God created a way for Adam and Eve to show their love and obedience to Him. In the wonderful garden, God created an "off limits" zone. It was a tree. If you are familiar with the Bible, you know trees have a lot of significance with God. Adam and Eve were not to touch this particular tree. It was named "*the tree of the knowledge of good and evil*" (Geneses 2:17). Every other tree was okay, excluding this one. God told Adam not to eat of this one tree. If Adam and Eve did eat from it, the result would be death.

The enemy of the souls of men, Satan, in the form of a serpent, began planning his attack. He centered his plan at the point of Adam and Eve's opportunity to show their obedience—the tree of the knowledge of good and evil. Satan's plan was not an attack on Adam. Adam heard from God in person about the forbidden fruit—there was no room for doubt in his mind. Rather, Satan beguiled Eve, who only heard the second-hand rule about the forbidden fruit. Satan hates first-hand, eyewitness accounts. He can't compete with a concrete testimony.

Satan asked Eve to try the forbidden fruit. Eve attempted to quote Adam, *"But of the fruit of the tree which is in the midst of the garden, God hath said, Ye shall not eat of it, neither shall ye touch it, lest ye die"* (Geneses 3:3, 4). In response, the snake manipulated her words. *"And the serpent said unto the woman, Ye shall **not** surely die . . ."* He repeated her words, correcting her with his addition as if she forgot that one word.

Satan's extra one word caused Eve to fall prey to his deceptive ploy. From there, she persuaded Adam to follow. At this point in history, Satan introduced sin into the human race and set the stage for a tremendous magnitude of human suffering. Many attempt to blame God for all of the subsequent misfortune, but He is not to blame. Satan is to blame. Satan is the one who changed one simple word.

To provide a covering for Adam and Eve, God killed innocent animals to use their skins as clothing. In His justice, God required the consequences for sin. He evicted Adam and Eve from Eden, and the pain of sin entered their lives. They discovered the importance of obedience to God's specific plans in their unfortunate circumstances. They discovered the power of one word.

At this point in my research and preparing for court, I see the operating system the enemy uses against us. I wonder if I will see deception again as part of Satan's tactical pattern. He simply changed one word and deceived humanity. I wonder if deception through a small change may be his modus operandi.

CHAPTER 5

THE PAINTING

I'M NOT AN ARTIST. I can paint your house; however, I cannot paint your portrait. I appreciate art and the genius behind every brush stroke. But I'm very limited when it comes to creating art. So, as I stand in the National Art Museum, part of the Smithsonian Institute in Washington, D.C., I marvel at the bold paint daubs that comprise the unique painting before me. Blues, greens, yellows and reds mingle and dance together on the canvas.

I can almost smell the flowers, and jump into the unfathomable depths of the water. I am looking at Monet's "Water Lilies." It seems, the more pronounced the brush strokes on a particular canvas, the more valuable the work of art. Such images almost come to life.

In a flash, my mind's eye takes me to the image of another painter. This time, the brush is a hyssop branch held in the hand of a Hebrew householder. The pigment is fresh blood, the blood of a lamb. The canvas is not linen or primitive papyrus, but rather the doorpost and entryway of a humble home in Egypt.

It is the night of the Passover. According to the Biblical account in Exodus 12, the first Passover occurred some four hundred years after the fledgling nation of Israel came to Egypt to escape starvation. Today, they will escape death, and tomorrow they will escape slavery. In Egypt on Passover night, blood splotches, which mark every Jewish doorway in Goshen, will preserve life. The angelic spirit of death will pass through the land of Egypt and will spare the life of the firstborn only if the family applies the blood of the lamb to their home.

In future generations, a Jewish holiday will mark the Passover night, and people will remember its severity for centuries to come. The painting of blood on the door frame foreshadows the most valuable brush strokes that will ever appear in history. It is a hint of the sacrifice of Jesus Christ, when once again out of kindness toward humanity God will offer innocent blood to apply as a cover for our souls.

The blood on the doorposts paints a picture of love that unfolds through the life of Jesus Christ.

The sad mistake of Adam and Eve brought the bloodshed of innocent animals to provide a covering for them. Likewise, the animals slain in Goshen, Egypt provided a covering of protection from the death angel on the first Passover night. Even so, the shed blood of Jesus, the Lamb of God offers a covering for us and remits all our sins—past, present, and future.

The entire Exodus story is full of beautiful typology. Bondage in Egypt typifies our sinful existence as prisoners to Satan's rule. Escaping Egypt mirrors our conversion from sin to salvation; the crossing of the Red Sea is a picture of water baptism.

As I think of how the Israelites wandered in the wilderness, my mind goes to our lives as children of God. Our walk with the Lord is a spiritual pilgrimage, including trials and tribulations, and supported by daily provisions. The children of Israel had manna, quail, water from the rock, and protection of the cloud by day and the pillar of fire by night. They were preserved—no one was feeble among them, and their shoes and clothes did not wear out. Their journey is an amazing, wonderful illustration given to encourage us in our exodus from sin. Just as He did for them, God protects and provides for us in a spiritual sense.

But the most important typology in the Passover story was the blood. The blood on the doorposts paints a picture of love that unfolds through the life of Jesus Christ. There will be blood on another door. Jesus said, "*I am the door: by me if any man enters in, he shall be saved, and shall go in and out, and find pasture*" (John 10:9). There will be Blood from another Spotless Lamb, "*The Lamb slain from the foundation of the world*" (Revelation 13:8). The picture will come to life as the Lamb sheds His blood to purchase salvation for the souls of mankind. His sacrifice will fully pay for the sinful debt incurred as a result of Satan's deceit and humanity's disobedience.

There is nothing we need do, or can do, to add to the payment made by Jesus' precious blood to redeem us from our sinful state. The slain Lamb of God provides the full payment for our sins. It's our responsibility to choose to apply the blood of Christ to our lives and accept the gift of His Spirit.

Because God is a holy God, we call His Spirit the "Holy Spirit." On the third day after His cruel death on a Roman cross, Jesus rose from the dead, therefore some scriptures refer to the Holy Spirit as the "Holy Ghost."

In the Book of Acts, the recorded beginning of the New Testament Church, believers received the gift of the Holy Ghost for the first time. Astonished bystanders beheld the Power of God and asked what they should do. One obliging apostle of Jesus, Peter, stood and addressed the crowd. His answer was: *"Repent, and be baptized every one of you in the name of Jesus Christ for the remission of sins, and ye shall receive the gift of the Holy Ghost"* (Acts 2:38).

In Acts 2, the believers spoke in languages they did not know; it was the evidence of receiving the gift of the Holy Ghost. The gift is *"Christ in you, the hope of glory"* (Colossians 1:27). The gift of the Holy Ghost is the Comforter Jesus spoke of in the Gospel of John, Chapters 14, 15 and 16. In John 14:18, Jesus said, *"I will not leave you comfortless: I will come to you."*

We remain in awe of the Power of God. The opportunity to have the blood of the sinless Lamb provide remittance and remission of our sins overwhelms our comprehension. In Matthew 26:28, Jesus said, *"This is my blood . . . Shed for many for the remission of sins."*

Remission comes through the shedding of blood. The blood of Whom? The Lamb! Who was the Lamb? Jesus! So, now we stand face to face with the Gospel of Christ: the death, burial and resurrection of Jesus Christ. Jesus, the Messiah, came to save us from our human tragedy. He purchased our salvation through His blood; the blood of Jesus saves us.

So, blood was shed for Adam and Eve in the garden. It was shed for the nation of Israel in Goshen ahead of their exodus from Egypt, with all its typology. And blood was shed at Calvary to cleanse us all from sin.

2 Thessalonians 1:8 states we must obey the Gospel to escape punishment. Isn't the Gospel the "good news" of the death, burial, and resurrection of Jesus? How can we obey the Gospel? The Bible tells us what to do.

The first part of the Gospel is Jesus' death. We obey Jesus' death when we repent of our sins and die to sin. Repentance is the "death," and we must die daily (1 Corinthians 15:31). The second part of the Gospel is Jesus' burial. We obey His burial when we are baptized in water. Baptism is our spiritual "burial" (Romans 6:4 and Colossians 2:12). Then comes the third part of the Gospel, the "Resurrection." When we obey the resurrection of Jesus, we are raised from spiritual death into new life. The only power strong enough to raise us into new life is God's power—the Holy Spirit, or Holy Ghost. When we receive the gift of new life, we become a new creature and are "born again" (2 Corinthians 5:17).

In Romans 6:4, the Apostle Paul said, "*We are buried with Him by baptism into death: that like as Christ was raised from the dead by the glory of the Father, even so we also should walk in newness of life.*"

We are dependent on blood to purchase the remission of our sins. Jesus shed His blood as payment for our sins. We are buried *with Him* when we are baptized. After knowing all of this, it makes sense that Peter's instruction was for us to be baptized in Jesus' name. The blood of Jesus Christ is an integral part of the specific plan of salvation from a specific God! God paints the picture of incredible love throughout the Bible. His beautiful artistic work has been in the making since the foundation of the world (Revelation 13:8).

CHAPTER 6

THE FACTS, JUST THE FACTS

I'M INTERESTED IN THE FACTS that have a bearing on my soul, your soul, and the souls of everyone we love. We've already examined the weight of eternity, the fact that God is specific and gives us clear instructions, and that Satan has experience in making slight and subtle changes to God's divine plan.

The voice we can trust is the Holy Bible—God's written Word. God provides the salvation plan in His Word, and we know baptism is a part of the plan. Let's take a look at baptismal practices in the church today and hold them up to the most powerful Evidence we have—God's Word.

There are millions of wonderful people in the world today who have experienced water baptism with the following words spoken over them: "In the name of the Father, and of the Son, and of the Holy Ghost." This common baptismal formula is based on Matthew 28:19, where Jesus said, *"Go ye therefore, and teach all nations, baptizing them in the* name *of the Father, and of the Son, and of the Holy Ghost."*

This verse is often interpreted in a different way than the early church saw it. In light of the verse we just read, it is both interesting and puzzling to me that the Bible records early believers baptizing in the singular name of "Jesus." I must find an explanation for why there was a change in baptismal method from the early Christian church to what many practice today. When did the baptismal formula change, and how did that new mode become so widespread?

After Jesus' recorded words in Matthew 28:19, every baptism recorded in the Bible was performed in Jesus Name. If the Apostle Peter heard Jesus say to baptize "in the name of the Father, Son, and Holy Ghost," why then did Peter preach that believers were to be baptized in Jesus' Name (Acts 2:38)?

I've heard many great people say, "I would rather take the words of Jesus than to take the words of Peter." When we study the scriptures, however, both Jesus and Peter were actually saying the same thing. In fact, if the Bible were truly conflicting in these two passages, we would have major issues with Biblical accuracy.

It was not a major change. Just enough change to effectively disconnect humanity from the Power won on Calvary's Cross.

Frankly, if you are still primarily interested in the words of Jesus think of His statement in Luke 24:47. *"And that repentance and remission of sins should be preached in **his name** among all nations, beginning at Jerusalem."* I know it sounds as though someone else is speaking of Jesus in this passage, but Jesus is quoting Old Testament prophecy about Himself. In a red-letter edition of The Bible, the verse is red. Check it out. Some Bibles even reference Matthew 28:19 and Luke 24:47 to each other; they are referencing the same story told by two different authors. Studying these two scriptures along with Acts 2:38, allows us to see a common denominator. Each verse refers to a singular "name." One Name. That Name belongs to the One who bled and died, Jesus.

It's a Biblical fact; the New Testament Church baptized in the name of Jesus. Here is a list of scriptures that illustrate the only baptismal mode used by the New Testament Church.

Acts 8:16, *"For as yet he was fallen upon none of them: only they were baptized in the name of the Lord Jesus."*

Acts 10:48, *"And he commanded them to be baptized in the name of the Lord. Then prayed they him to tarry certain days."*

Acts 19:5, *"When they heard this, they were baptized in the name of the Lord Jesus."*

Acts 22:16, *"And now why tarriest thou? Arise, and be baptized, and wash away thy sins, calling on the name of the Lord."*

We've examined the Evidence in God's Word. We know the facts, but we're still missing a piece of the puzzle. What happened to change the baptismal formula? We must present more facts. There is no Biblical reference to the change in baptismal mode from "Jesus Name" into what often is used today, "the name of the Father, Son, and Holy Ghost." To

When did the baptismal formula change, and how did that new mode become so widespread?

identify the point of change, we must look at the facts presented in accounts of religious history outside of the

Bible.

There's no better place for facts than a courtroom. In the next chapter, we will begin a trial of eternal proportions. But first, allow me to set the stage.

WE ENTER
THE COURT OF ETERNAL AFFAIRS

Satan, the enemy of our souls, is charged with subverting the Truth of the Gospel. It was not a major change. Just enough change to effectively disconnect humanity from the Power won on Calvary's Cross. He changed one word (one Name) in God's specific plan for mankind's salvation. It was enough to derail the redemption plan, but not enough for humankind to depart from religion. He didn't try to cause general alarm but simply made a slight shift. Just like in the Garden; Satan didn't say, "God didn't speak to you and Adam." He just in essence said, "You misunderstood."

You have a role to play in the Court of Eternal Affairs as well. You are hereby summoned to jury duty. Use your imagination to visualize and illuminate the facts as I call on various historic figures to testify under oath. The court will examine the events and personalities surrounding changes in church practices concerning baptism. Let there be truth, the whole truth, and nothing but the truth—affirmed by Almighty God.

PART 2

THE COURT
OF ETERNAL AFFAIRS

CHAPTER 7

THE FIRST WITNESS

A VISIT TO

THE COURTROOM IN

MY OLD HOMETOWN

AS I SIT IN THE COURTROOM of an Honorable Federal Judge, I admire the intricate and handsome woodwork of the polished panels behind the judge's desk. This building has a unique smell. It is the same smell it had when I came here as a child. My mother would bring me with her to this courthouse to mail packages at the Post Office, which was on the first floor.

I well remember the gentleman who operated the small concession counter there. He was blind, but in spite of his disability he was always pleasant. I was amazed at his ability to count back our change accurately when we would purchase gum or a candy bar.

Today I am at the courthouse responding to a summons to appear for Federal Jury Duty. It's a first for me. Another first will come later today when I will be elected to public office: Foreman of the Jury.

I won't give the details of the case proceedings we dealt with that day, but one interesting fact bears sharing. It is about the defense attorney. During the voir dire, when prospective jurors answer questions, the defense attorney made a statement that essentially conceded the guilt of his client. I don't think he ever realized the impact of what he said. The trial didn't turn out too well for his client.

WE RE-ENTER
THE COURT OF ETERNAL AFFAIRS

Now our attention is called to another courtroom—an imaginary place full of real people from history, all relevant to the important subject at hand. The defendant is Satan, and he is charged with perverting the Truth of The Gospel of Christ. The gravity of the situation weighs on everyone in the room. Every soul's eternal destiny depends on the redeeming Blood of Jesus Christ—that's why it's so important to know the Truth.

In the criminal charge of perverting truth, Satan is accused of tampering with the plan of God to prevent the power of the Blood of Jesus from effectively prevailing in the lives of believers. By removing the specific Name of Jesus from baptism, the archenemy of our souls did everything he could to prevent our personal connection with remission, or forgiveness, for sin.

At first glance, changing the baptismal formula seems but a small thing, but remember it doesn't require much temperature change before Edison's light bulb darkens, and Fulton's steamboat sits idle. Satan's offense is great. He deceives many into believing it isn't important to call on the Name of Jesus in baptism. Jesus—this is the Name of the One that shed His

Every soul's eternal destiny depends on the redeeming Blood of Jesus Christ—that's why it's so important to know the Truth.

Blood to pay the price for the remission of sin.

The courtroom falls silent as all rise, and the jury is sworn in. A court official gives instructions to the jury. "Forget anything you have heard that may bias your judgment of the facts presented. The truth is all you are interested in at this time." *As a member of the jury, the instruction is for you, my reader.*

WITNESS NUMBER ONE

Our first witness is called to the stand: an overbearing and egotistical world leader well known to historians. His name is Nero. As a part of the current legal proceedings, Nero is a minor player. Though guilty of many heinous crimes against humanity, and headed for a judgment trial himself, at this time he is only a witness. He is called to testify about his role in setting the stage for the downward spiral against the Roman Empire, which led to political corruption of the church and eventual doctrinal perversion.

I am the only attorney present—the Prosecutor. There is no attorney willing to provide defense for the devil. I approach the stand, address the witness and the interrogation begins.

"Be seated. Please state your name for the court."

"My name is Nero, Emperor of Rome."

"You were The Roman Emperor during what time in history?"

"AD 54 to 68. 14 years."

"Is it true that you consider yourself not only one of Rome's grandest emperors but also an accomplished performer of the arts? A singer, musician and poet?"

"Oh, yes, indeed!"

"Are you aware that many of your subjects did not relish your music and poetry? That they were forced to sit and endure it as you entertained?"

"Well, you know, some people don't appreciate the arts. They must be forced to cultivate a taste for finer performances."

"Aren't you the Roman Emperor responsible for the martyrdom of most of the Apostles of Jesus Christ?" I ask the man sitting before me.

"Yes. It was my pleasure. As you probably know, they believed in only one God. We Romans wisely acknowledge many gods."

"Is it true that you found Rome so despicable that you wanted to totally rebuild it?"

"Yes. It was dirty, disgusting and disorganized."

"So you deliberately set fire to burn Rome to the ground?"

"Well, yes."

"And did you stand in your tower and play the lyre while you watched Rome burn?"

"Yes, it is true, but, well, I can't remember exactly what instrument I was playing. Rome needed to burn so I could rebuild and improve it. It was worth celebrating with music."

"Is it also true that because of heated accusation against yourself as being guilty of arson, you blamed the Christians of Rome for setting the fire just to save your skin?"

"Yes, but it didn't hurt anything. I considered the Christians to be lunatics anyway."

"How many Roman Christians died because of your

false accusation?"

"I don't know exactly. It was in the thousands, but they weren't important to me."

"Is it true that you killed some Christians by coating their clothes with wax and burning them at the stake in your courtyard just to illuminate your festivities at night? And, also, that some of them were sewn up in animal skins and thrown before packs of wild dogs in the Coliseum?"

"Yes, all true."

"No further questions. Step down."

At this point, the jury is going to recess. Many jurors are queasy and nauseated after hearing the witness testify about his role in persecuting Christians and setting the cultural stage against them.

CHAPTER 8
A NEW WORD

AS THE JURY returns to their seats, I again address the Court of Eternal Affairs in my role as Prosecuting Council. "Before I call my next witness to the Court of Eternal Affairs, I would like to present historic evidence to continue building my case."

The Spirit of Truth agrees and gives permission. "You may proceed."

"In the flourishing first century or two of the fledgling New Testament Church," I begin, "there was wildfire-like growth in the faith. In spite of persecution, the reality of an intimate relationship with the very God of the universe drew multitudes to Christian conversion. They converted from Judaism, Greek Mythology, worship of Baal and other idols, and whatever other forms of religion were present and prevalent at the time.

"As with any change, there were growing pains. The scarce accessibility to written scripture was the Achilles heel of the young body of believers. The New Testament was only recently written, making it relatively unavailable for study. People who followed the Jewish culture actively committed Old Testament scripture to memory, but Gentiles didn't have that foundational understanding. Greek philosophy and other Gentile influences began conjuring legend concerning New Testament scripture. Over time, half-truths mixed with legend began to challenge the accuracy of Christian recollection.

"Trouble began to brew as Satan's forces took advantage of Christian converts' understanding. There is danger anytime a believer is unsure of the Word of God. Just like the deception in the Garden of Eden, Satan began to twist parts of God's Word a second time around.

"Because of conflicting viewpoints, a clamor of discord and disagreement among bishops, clergy, and general church leadership arose to a great magnitude. The subject was Christology. They were arguing about who Jesus was. Plato, the famed Greek philosopher, perpetuated a part of the initial fuel of the furor."

WITNESS TWO

"And so, I call my next witness—Plato—to the stand."

Voices hush to whispers throughout the courtroom as Plato enters and takes the witness stand.

"Do you swear to tell the truth, the whole truth and nothing but the truth?"

"I do," Plato says.

The questioning begins. "You were and are a very influential man," I say. "People have studied your thoughts and teachings for hundreds of years. You had a unique view of the God of Israel. Can you explain your position and reasoning?"

"Of course I can! A God as mighty as Jehovah God of Israel, or at least as great as He was described to be, is surely untouchable. God is so high above all; it is logically impossible for such a mighty God to endure the mortal suffering and death Jesus experienced," Plato explains. "Jesus' claim to be God is outlandish to say the least."

"So, you're saying Jesus claimed to be God? Can you clarify?" I ask.

"Even though Jesus Himself told His disciples He was God Almighty in the flesh, as recorded in John 14:9, it would be impossible for Almighty God to live in a human body. The believers claim God prepared a body—Jesus—specifically for sacrifice. The reference for that idea is Hebrews 10:5. John the Baptist claimed Jesus was the Lamb of God who came to take away the sins of the world, as recorded in John 1:29. As the Lamb of God, Jesus supposedly shed His life-blood for our sins. That is all impossible, of course."

"Sir, are you or your contemporaries clergyman?"

"No, I'm not a clergyman. I'm a philosopher, as are my associates."

"Do you believe in God?"

"I believe in gods, of course—Greek gods."

"Can you tell the court about these gods?"

"Greeks worship many gods. Some are gods of materialism, sensuality, and the human form. Others are gods of Greek mythology. We often worship them as triad gods, as we Greeks tend to see deity in groups of three."

"Did Christian church leaders after your time listen to your thoughts and ideas?"

"Yes. You said it yourself; I'm a very influential man."

"Are you aware that Christian arguments came about many years later as a direct result of your influence?"

"That's nice to know," Plato said smugly.

"That is all. Please step down. I call my next witness."

THE THIRD WITNESS

As the next witness walks to the stand, I begin the next set of questions. "Please state your name, when you lived, and a little bit about yourself for the court."

"My name is Iamblichus, and I am of the Alexandrian School of Philosophy. We are students of Plato, who began this institution some six hundred years earlier. I lived during the third century AD, or as some now refer to as CE or current era."

"I understand there were many so-called Christian leaders during your time who were influenced by Greek philosophy and some of Plato's ideas from many years prior. What occurred within the Christian church as a result of the influence of Greek philosophy?"

"It spurred obsession with the 'Christology' upheaval," Iamblichus responds. "It was also referred to as the Arian controversy because of the vocal part the church leader Arius played in the dispute."

"Can you explain to the court what Christology is, in layman's terms?"

"It's the study of Christ. It examined Christ's humanity and supposed deity, life and miracles. People began asking questions about who Jesus was. Was Jesus a 'Junior' God? Or, did God adopt Jesus as a son? Was He a separate person, but equal with God? Or, was He God?"

"I see. Can you explain your personal beliefs on the matter?" I ask.

"Yes, but you might not understand it. First, according to Neoplatonic reasoning, I saw the God of Israel as the transcendent incommunicable One. Also, in addition to this absolute One, I saw a second superexistant One, to stand between the absolute One and the many, as the producer of intellect. This is the initial dyad or duo. In addition to these, we added and assigned to a third rank the Demiurge or Creator-God, the Logos, thus creating a triad or triplicate god-aspect.

"You admit they crucified Jesus for His claim to be God, and then later you deny His very claim."

This closely follows Neoplatonism and its thoughts," Iamblichus attempts to explain as he quickly speaks.

"If Jesus were God, it would be impossible for him to suffer death, which was Plato's argument," he continues. "So, you see, One who is incommunicable; then, One who produces intellect; and also One who is the creator."

"This is all very confusing and not at all consistent with Biblical accounts of God," I say. "What do you have to say about that?"

"Well, it is very hard to comprehend it all."

"It would seem, according to your written work, *Theurgia*, you have incorporated the Assyrian-Chaldean plan of divine order of threes, a bit of Zoroastrianism, some Hinduism and the Egyptian worship of Amun into a blur of confusion," I say.

"As a matter of fact, all those influences do contribute in our philosophical effort to understand divinity," Iamblichus admits.

"Thank you for showing us how confused you philosophers actually were," I say. "Are you aware that the Apostle Paul predicted the Christology debate as he wrote to the Colossian believers? He wrote, *'Beware lest any man spoil you through philosophy and vain deceit, after the tradition of men, after the rudiments of the world, and not after Christ.'* It's recorded in Colossians 2:8."

"I've read it."

"It seems the Christology discussions themselves uncover a glaring irony. Had Jesus been only a junior God, or an adopted son, He would never have been crucified. Can you tell the court why Jesus was killed?"

"Jesus died as a result of His claim to be God Almighty in the flesh," Iamblichus says.

"As Jesus' words are recorded in Luke 11:20, *'But if I with the finger of God cast out devils, no doubt the kingdom of God is come upon you.'* In John 10:30 and 33, Jesus states, *'I and my Father are one. The Jews answered him, saying, For a good work we stone thee not; but for blasphemy; and because that thou, being a man, makest thyself God.'*

"To the Jews, it was a very serious offense for Christ to claim He was God manifest in the flesh. Why else would they have crucified Jesus?" I ask.

"That was the reason—He died because He claimed to be God," Iamblichus says.

"You've said why He was crucified, yet history tells us that in 300 short years, theologians influenced by Greek philosophy lost sight of what, in essence, actually brought about the death of Jesus. As you concur, He was crucified because He claimed to be God in human form. Religious leaders wanted Him executed because of His claim to be God. And it was all a part of God's plan to provide the perfect sacrifice for humanity's sins.

"Scripture tells us He was the express image of God

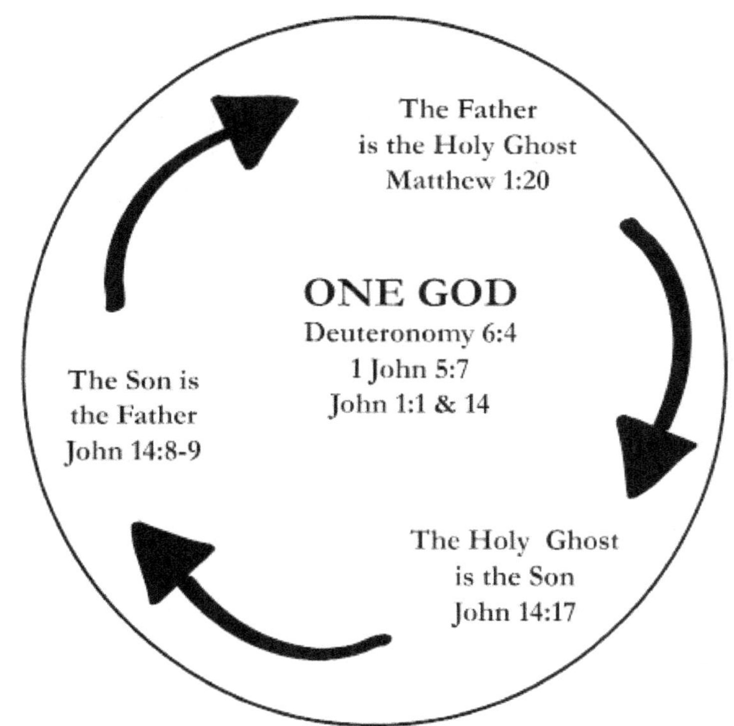

(Hebrews 1:3 and Colossians 1:15). What irony, indeed. You admit they crucified Jesus for His claim to be God, and then later you deny His very claim."

I turn to the jury and announce my next course of action. "Before I end my questions with this witness, I have a few other things to explore, especially considering the fact that he follows so closely with the thoughts of Plato, which had a heavy bearing on changes to baptismal practice. I present Exhibit 1, a scripture flow chart."

I unveil my chart and display it on an easel.

"This chart features three Bible verses in a circle formation, with an arrow between each verse. The first verse is Matthew 1:20, which illustrates that the Father is the Holy Ghost," I explain.

"*But while he thought on these things, behold, the angel of the Lord appeared unto him in a dream, saying, Joseph, thou son of David, fear not to take unto thee Mary thy wife; for that which is conceived in her is of the Holy Ghost.*'

"The second verse is John 14:17, which illustrates that the Holy Ghost is the Son. '*Even the Spirit of truth; whom the world cannot receive, because it seeth him not, neither knoweth him; but ye know him; for he dwelleth with you, and shall be in you.*'

"The third verse is John 14:8-9, which illustrates that the Son is the Father. '*Philip saith unto him, Lord, shew us the Father, and it sufficeth us. Jesus saith unto him, Have I been so long time with you, and yet hast thou not known me, Philip? he that hath seen me hath seen the Father; and how sayest thou then, shew us the Father?*'

"The scriptures confirm there is only one God. Just as the chart flows in a continuous circle, there is no break or separation between the Father, Son and Holy Ghost. In the center of the circle are another four verse references. Deuteronomy 6:4, which says, '*Hear, O Israel: the LORD our God is one LORD.*' 1 John 5:7, "*There are three that bear record in heaven, the Father, the Word, and the Holy Ghost: and these three are one.*' And John 1:1 and 14, '*In the beginning was the Word, and the Word was with God, and the Word was God. And the Word was made flesh and dwelt among*

It seems the Apostles would have known who Jesus was and have been better versed on what He taught than a lawyer born 200 years later.

us, (and we beheld his glory, the glory as of the only begotten of the Father,) full of grace and truth.'"

I turn and face my witness.

"Iamblichus, I point your attention to the chart displayed for the court. Please read the displayed scriptures and tell me if these are bona-fide references to the Holy Bible."

"Yes they are true scriptures from the Bible," he says.

"Do the three scriptures actually refer to the same person, Jesus Christ?" I ask.

"Yes, they do."

"Thank you. According to these verses, the terms Father, Son and Holy Ghost are all used interchangeably, referring to One God.

"Matthew 1:20, says the Holy Ghost is Jesus' Father. Then in John 14:8-9, Jesus stated we see the Father (the Holy Ghost) when we see Him.

"In John 14:17, we see Jesus dwell with us on the earth and later would be the One to live in us, as we know first happened in Acts 2.

"The Neoplatonic theory of three distinct persons of the godhead is erroneous. According to these verses there is only One God, and His Name is Jesus. John 8:24 specifically points to your error when Jesus says, *'For if you believe not that I am he, ye shall die in your sins.'*

"That's pretty strong language, but it plainly shows Jesus didn't want you to be eternally lost. Wouldn't you agree?"

Iamblichus nods in agreement.

At this point the court reporter throws a hand in the air and interjects to the witness, "Please speak clearly and plainly for the court, if you will."

Iamblichus complied. "Yes, the answer is yes," he said. "You may step down. I call my next witness for the day."

WITNESS NUMBER FOUR

"Please state your full name for the court."

"Quintus Septimius Florens Tertullianus. The Anglicans just call me Tertullian."

"What year were you born, and where?"

"160 AD. In Carthage, the Northern Roman province in Africa."

"Your occupation, sir?"

"I was trained and served as a lawyer."

"I see. As you know, usually when there is a shift in culture, society will invent new words to solidify new culture. For example, Shakespeare coined the word *addiction* in the 1600s. *Genocide* became part of our vocabulary in 1944. *Selfie* became a word in 2003. The invention of words is not a new phenomenon. Were people coining words in your time?" I ask.

"Yes. In fact, I coined a few myself," Tertullian says.

"Is it true that you are credited with coining a new term to describe the emerging philosophy of 'Three Persons, One Substance' in reference to the 'Christology' of Jesus Christ?"

"Yes."

"Would you please plainly state for the record of the court what that new word was?"

"Certainly, the word is *trinity*."

"Are you aware that this new word, *trinity*, gave tremendous substance to a concept so flawed it had been argued over since the church dignitary Montanus introduced it in 156 AD? Had the concept of the trinity been the prevailing thought in 33 AD, would it have watered down Jesus' identity so much that He would never have been crucified?"

"Possibly. I never thought about it that way . . . "

"Many wonder how you would come to know more about the affairs of Jesus than His Apostles, who were eyewitnesses to His life. It seems the Apostles would have known who Jesus was and would have been better versed on what He taught than a lawyer born 200 years later. Would you agree?"

"I am not going to answer that," Tertullian said.

"This witness doesn't want to incriminate himself. No further questions."

CHAPTER 9
CONSEQUENCES

THERE IT IS AGAIN. It is the sound of music. No, not the Broadway musical about a war-torn European family; this music concerns three young scientists—at least that's what we would call them in today's world. They, however, live in ancient Babylon.

We affectionately call these young men "The Three Hebrew Children." Their names, listed in Daniel 1:7, appear in Hebrew as well as Chaldean. Hananiah was called Shadrach. Mishael was named Meshach, and Azariah took on the name Abednego. Each name is hard to pronounce and is even more difficult to spell.

These three young men are prisoners of war. Forcibly taken from their homes in Jerusalem and brought all the way to Babylon, they find themselves in Nebuchadnezzar's powerful kingdom in 600 BC. They are among Israel's top students—the cream of the crop. Their incredible gifts and talents spared their lives. All the common folk among the Israelites are now either slaves, dead, or left for dead in the destroyed city of Jerusalem.

These three young men are extraordinary captives. They are considered leaders of their people. Brought to the king's palace to learn Babylonian ways, these boys are to help the Babylonians communicate with their new Israelite slaves and to help their people assimilate into their new world. Eventually, the three Hebrew boys are promoted to overseers in Babylon. Pretty high ranking for captives, don't you think? Their friend, Daniel, recommended them for the cushy job after he won the favor of King

Nebuchadnezzar by interpreting a dream.

Back to the music. It was "religious" music, meant to signal everyone to fall down and worship. Here's where the problem comes in. The object the Babylonians are worshiping is a golden image, a false god. The three Hebrews can't bow down to a false god; it goes against everything they believe. They risk their lives and disobey the command to bow.

King Nebuchadnezzar is mad. He is so proud of the newly sculpted golden image. The "reward" for refusing to worship the idol is death by the fiery furnace. As the three Hebrew men refuse to worship the idol, they are sentenced to burn in the furnace, in this case heated seven times hotter than normal. The soldiers who throw them into the furnace die as they come close to the intense heat.

Miraculously, the Hebrews are spared from death in the roaring flames. Not a hair on their heads is scorched. The smell of smoke doesn't even penetrate their clothes. How can it be? They live because they aren't in the fire alone. A fourth person accompanies them in the inferno. Old King Nebuchadnezzar says the extra person in the furnace looks like the "Son of God." Amazing.

The point of me sharing this story is that a person doesn't have to be in the wrong to be the recipient of harsh consequences. If we refuse to change our moral values and beliefs along with cultural shifts, the gap between where we Christians have always held our ground and where the world around us stands will grow wider. A cultural movement can put us at odds with society and human authority.

As we go back to The Court of Eternal Affairs, it seems our next witness is also a victim of negative cultural shift.

EXCOMMUNICATED

"Please be seated. State your name for the court."

"My name is Sabellius."

"Were you, Sabellius, a minister of the Gospel of Christ in 220 AD?

"Yes, I was."

"And during your ministry, did you oppose the new doctrine of the trinity, and the developing views on Christology?"

"Yes, I did oppose the development of the trinity during the time Tertullian and Hippolytus introduced it between 180 AD and 220 AD."

"Is it true you lost fellowship with the ministers you had served with for many years, all because you refused to change your beliefs and accept the new trinity doctrine?"

"Yes, that is true."

"History records that your beliefs about God in the early third century AD are very similar to the current Christian churches who baptize in the Name of Jesus, and believe that God successively revealed Himself to humanity as the Father in creation, the Son in redemption and the Spirit in sanctification and regeneration. Do you agree?"

"Yes, history is correct on that. My position that there is only one God, who reveals Himself to humanity over time, is scriptural.

"As 1 Timothy 3:16 states, *'And without controversy great is the mystery of godliness: God was manifest in the flesh, justified in the Spirit, seen of angels, preached unto the Gentiles, believed on in the world, received up into glory.'*

"As well, John 14:17 states, *'Even the Spirit of truth; whom the world cannot receive, because it seeth him not, neither knoweth him: but ye know him; for he dwelleth with you, and shall be in you.'*"

"Thank you, no further questions."

CHAPTER 10

THE COUNCIL

THE YEAR IS 325 A.D.

The place is Constantinople—the revolving doorway of travel, trade routes and the link between the East and West. It's the new headquarters of the Roman Empire. In modern times, we would know this city as Istanbul, Turkey.

The current Roman Emperor, Constantine, for whom the city is named, is an adept opportunist bent on advancing his world enterprise. He will take any avenue available to strengthen his power. He sees an opportunity in a conflict amongst Christians, a faith that is only about 300 years old. There is a growing upheaval of dialog about who Jesus was. The Roman Emperor believes he sees a way to marry his empire to the growing, but newly conflicted, religion. In doing so, he might just renew and expand the reach of his failing empire.

At Constantine's persuasive invitation, 318 bishops and Christian Church dignitaries convene at his summer home in the little town of Nicaea, just a few miles southwest of Constantinople. Official Roman ships, carriages, and coaches dispatch to collect and deliver the host of religious delegates to the first-ever global church council. Who could resist a compelling Emperor? After all, he is providing complimentary transportation, food and lodging for the month-long council.

And, if all his hospitality seemed extremely benevolent, his gifts were modestly offset only by his insistence on facilitating and moderating the proceedings. Politics and church leadership, who said they couldn't mix? Though in actuality a pagan priest, Constantine became known as "the Bishop of Bishops" as he ineptly presided over the Council of Nicaea. His Christian authority was nothing but a farce.

The first world council began, and the Christology debate, heated by opinion and ego, mushroomed among bishops and clergymen. Faith-fueled turmoil creates the perfect storm. Some of the religious leaders came to fisticuffs. As with many issues that involve great pools of society, shrewd politicians often see opportunity in the making within the religious realm, and the Emperor played his cards to win.

THE ROYAL WITNESS

The chamber falls silent as the bailiff calls for yet another Roman Emperor to come to the witness stand. There is pomp and flourish in the court as the man enters the room. The witness takes his seat, as I begin my examination.

"Please state for the court your name and office."

"My name is Constantine the Great, and I served as emperor of the Roman Empire from AD 306 until 337."

"Thank you, and now just a few questions. First of all, as Emperor of Rome did you have family members, including one of your sons, killed to preserve your continuance as emperor?"

"Yes, it is true. Sometimes the good of the empire takes precedence over all else."

"Is it also true that you held the office of priest in the pagan religious system of Rome?" I ask.

"Yes."

"As such, did you relish the idea of becoming a pagan deity after death so that people would worship you as a Roman God?"

"That was attractive to me. It was my eternal goal."

"Tell us a little about the pagan practices in Rome. What were they like?"

"We were polytheist, with a reverence for nature and animal worship. We served many gods simultaneously, the gods of earth, air, fire and water, alongside pantheon gods from the distant past," Constantine said.

"Many pagans of your day believed in reincarnation as well as occasional human sacrifice. Were you ever involved in sacrificing a human?"

"Well, like you mentioned, I did believe in reincarnation. It wasn't as if the sacrificed ones wouldn't be reborn."

"Please answer the question directly."

"Yes. I have nothing to be ashamed of," he said. "They were reborn into a better life in my view."

"Is there any truth to the historic account of your conversion to Christianity, which states your public confession of belief was primarily for show and political reasons?"

"Yes, I used my posed alliance with Christianity for political gain. I was not baptized as a Christian follower until I was at the point of death," Constantine admitted. "That's when some of the other Christians realized I had never been baptized."

"Historians report that you sponsored the Council of Nicaea for political reasons. Is that true?"

"Yes. I used the growing Christology conflict as a tool to advance the Roman Empire."

"Can you explain what happened at the Council of Nicaea?"

"I brought bishops and clergy together for a month-long conference, at my expense, to discuss matters of global importance," Constantine says smugly.

"Did you plan to take advantage of whatever agreement they would arrive at, for the growth of your empire?"

"Of course. Why wouldn't I? What a golden opportunity."

"Did you care how the religious leaders resolved the Christology issue?"

"No. It didn't matter what they agreed on, as long as it would benefit Rome. I attached Roman sponsorship to the decision to heighten the growth of my Empire."

"I see. Did you see sponsoring the Council as an opportunity to enhance your fame as emperor?"

"Yes. Anything to turn people back to me—er, Rome."

"Did you threaten persecution to Christians who disagreed with the Council's newly established creed?"

"Of course, any dissenters must be kept in line. Why should they balk? Their leaders made the decrees. If they can't fall in line, they are obviously the rebel type."

"To make all of the information clear to the jury, I will summarize what we've established. You, Constantine, killed your son for political power. You were a pagan priest and a fake Christian. You devised the Nicene Council in 325 AD to take advantage of the Christology conflict, which developed in the second century New Testament Church.

"You had no real interest in how they resolved the conflict, as long as you could use the new accord to enhance the image of the failing Roman Empire. Your intent was to use church growth to assure growth for your empire by state sponsorship of the restructured church.

"You further promoted the new religious creed by threatening persecution to those who did not adhere to it. Anyone who did not agree became known as a heretic. The infamous persecution was said to be equally as severe as previous punishments were toward Christians of prior years. In other words, where early Christians feared severe persecution, torture, and death, now *non-subscribers* of the new Roman-sponsored church would face equally severe action if they did not adhere to the newly formulated dictates.

"Is all that I said accurate?"

"That is an accurate summary of my testimony to what happened during my reign," Constantine agrees.

"One final question: what was the name of the new Roman version of the Christian movement?"

"The Roman Catholic Church, of course."

"Thank you. No further questions. You may step down."

I turn toward the jury members and make a final statement as the witness steps down.

"Members of the jury, we have just uncovered the underlying cause of widespread false doctrine. The trinitarian teachings, beliefs and baptismal practices are unbiblical lingering remnants of the influence of the Roman Empire."

CHAPTER 11

HIJACKED

ON JULY 16, 1948, a Cathay Pacific Airways twin-engine seaplane took off from the Portuguese colony of Macau. The plane, dubbed "Miss Maca," flew over the water and headed for Hong Kong some 38 miles away. It was a regular flight, which often carried gold bullion as its cargo.

As a commercial flight, there were 23 passengers aboard, most of them wealthy. While the plane was still gaining initial altitude, one passenger, a part of a four-person gang that boarded the flight carrying handguns, demanded the pilot surrender control of the aircraft to him. A fight broke out in the cockpit of the seaplane, and the hijacker shot and killed the pilot and co-pilot. With the body of the pilot slumped over at the controls, the aircraft began a severe nosedive and crashed into the China Sea.

Fishermen found Wong Yu, the sole survivor of the disaster. They admitted him to the hospital due to injuries sustained in the crash. After some time, Wong confided to another patient that he was the mastermind of the hijacking attempt. Little did he know, but the other "patient" was a police detective. Wong Yu's confession solved the mystery of what brought the flight to such a prompt and tragic end. Miss Maca went down in history as the world's first hijacked commercial flight. But, as we all know, it would be far from the last.

A hijacking event usually involves taking over controls and changing the direction and destination of the vehicle. Sadly, hijackings often end tragically. The great majority of people severely affected are simply along for the ride.

In the preceding court testimonials, we witnessed the attempt of Satan, the enemy of our souls, to hijack New Testament church doctrine through secular government force. He set about to derail the very foundation of the Gospel, to bypass the effective power of the blood of Jesus Christ by omitting the Name of Jesus from baptism. The hijacking involved high stakes: the souls of millions along for the ride of life, trusting in human pilots flying the religion plane.

The Roman Empire took third century Christians into its clutches, formulating the Roman version of the Christian movement—the Roman Catholic Church. They removed the Biblical doctrinal stance that Jesus is God manifest in the flesh, and initiated a new baptismal formula. The Roman Catholic Church no longer invoked the Name of Jesus. The domino effect was that the Blood of Jesus was not spiritually applied to the soul at baptism.

Discussion and dispute over who Jesus was (the Christology/Arian debate) paved the way to usher out the most wonderful Name of Jesus from the baptismal equation. Ironically, when believers prayed for the sick they still called on the healing Name of Jesus. They still exorcised demons in the powerful Name of Jesus. However, when it came to baptism (the point where the Blood is applied to the soul of man) the new Roman Catholic Church conceded and dropped the Name above all Names.

It was just a small change, but it had massive consequences.

Their actions demonstrate a chilling parallel to Jesus' words in Matthew 7:22-23, *"Many will say to me in that day, Lord, Lord, have we not prophesied in thy name? and in thy name have cast out devils? and in thy name done many wonderful works? And then will I profess unto them, I never knew you: depart from me, ye that work iniquity."*

They began to baptize in the trinitarian formula, which reflected the influence of Greek paganism's belief in triad deity. Their faulty interpretation of Matthew 28:19 reflects the new tradition.

It was just a small change, but it had massive consequences. Baptism left the Biblical formula and was now erroneously administered under a series of titles. They began leaving off the wonderful Name of Jesus, the name of the very one who shed the atoning, redeeming blood to save us. They began to violate Colossians 3:17, *"Whatsoever ye do in word or deed, do all in the name of the Lord Jesus . . ."*

We must return to the devil's hijacking plot. Fast forward. History illustrates some 1200 years of varying degrees of secular Roman influence on the church. Finally, the Reformation began in the 1500's.

The major impetus for the Reformation had to do with resentment over financial issues concerning the Roman Catholic Church. Indulgences, or the monetary purchase of the opportunity to indulge in some wrongdoing, were commonplace. The purchase of an indulgence gave a person permission to sin. Other blatant money issues revolved around the dead. Church officials extorted great sums of money from mourners in exchange for promising to move the departed loved one's soul out of purgatory and limbo to a more suitable eternal resting place, as if they had such power.

Even the priesthood was not exempt from financial corruption. Open vacancies for ministry went to the highest bidder. If a high tier position became available, a succession of priests and rectors, or their financiers, paid as much as a year's salary to obtain a better position with more power. A sort of musical chairs would follow.

Luther, Calvin, Zwingli, and Knox were fed up with monetary demands from the Roman Catholic Church. They protested, beginning the Protestant movement. With the organization of the Protestant movement, the group now had freedom from the monetary demands of the Catholic Church. They called themselves "reformed" but their theology and worship didn't change to any significant extent. Actually, among the reformers, there was strong resistance to change from the existing doctrinal structure that wrongly prevailed for 1200 years prior to the Reformation.

We can best illustrate their resistance to change by introducing you to one last witness in the Court of Eternal Affairs.

THE FINAL WITNESS

"Please state your name for the court."

"My name is Miguel Serveto Conesa in my native language, Spanish. Many know me by my Anglican name, Michael Servetus. I lived between AD 1511 and 1553."

"Besides being a theologian, you were also a physician, correct?" I ask my witness.

"Yes, among other things, I was a physician."

"What were some of those other things?"

"I was trained in mathematics, astronomy, meteorology, geography, pharmacology and jurisprudence. I was the first to describe the correct function of cardiopulmonary circulation, which is the circuit the blood makes through the lungs and the different chambers of the heart," Servetus says.

"Is it true, as a theologian, your attempt to correct an error from the Roman Catholic Church during the Reformation effort gained momentum?"

"Yes, I wrote a treatise on the error of the doctrine of the trinity."

"What did you experience as a result of your effort to bring Christianity back to its original belief?"

"I was condemned by the Roman Catholic Church as well as the Reformation group. They all stood together to defend the trinitarian belief, put in place in the third century."

"What was the outcome of the situation?"

"I was burnt at the stake, not by the Roman system that martyred so many reformers during the Inquisition, but by a reformer. He fueled the fire himself and used green wood so that I would suffer a slower and more agonizing death. Thankfully, I did have followers who continued to carry the message of the belief in only One God."

"Who was the reformer responsible for your death?"

"His name was John Calvin. History records the details for those who wish to know more. Too bad he did not later see the error of his ways. It is such a pity that the Reformation could not right the 1200-year-old false views of Christ and baptismal doctrine."

"Thank you for your testimony. No further questions for this witness."

CHAPTER 12

JURY DELIBERATION

BACK AT THE
HOMETOWN COURTHOUSE

THE LAWYERS make their arguments and final statements. The jury retires to deliberate. The bailiff locks the chamber door and we, the twelve citizens dedicated to justice, begin our discussions.

The trial took two days; the jury deliberation will take another three. We are required to have a unanimous verdict. All of us know the evidence says the defendant is guilty—all of us except for one.

The summary lies before us. We have evidence. We can read back over the transcripts. We have the court record at our disposal. We must make a decision, but we have our feelings to contend with.

For eleven of us, our feelings are not a problem. What we feel parallels with what we saw and heard. We jury members began with a blank slate and took in the information as it was presented—all of us except for one.

I will call her Mae.

Mae. Her experiences flash before her eyes. She suffered much wrong in her life. She is unsure on how she sees the evidence. The defense attorney who chose her for the jury panel chose well. Somehow he knew she had a past that could influence her decisions. Choosing Mae was about the only thing the defense attorney did well. Do you remember my account of his misstatement during the voir dire? To our credit, we don't take his word for guilt or innocence. We weigh the evidence.

But Mae isn't totally adamant the accused is innocent. She is just unsure of his guilt. It isn't that the prosecution failed to present a compelling case. Mae is unsure of her decision because of her unfortunate life experiences, which paint her view of the world.

Is Satan guilty of influencing church doctrine and baptismal practices?

Eleven of us reason with her. We go around the table to recount and recall the evidence. We stand together, and we stand firm, but Mae just can't see it.

We fall silent. We rest. We are polite. We wait.

After an hour or two of silence, Mae shoves her chair away from the table and shouts, "I see it! Now I see it!" That afternoon, on the third day of deliberations, our jury returns the unanimous verdict—"guilty."

CLOSING STATEMENTS AT
THE COURT OF ETERNAL AFFAIRS

Satan is on trial now. We all know he is guilty of much wrongdoing, but the question before you, members of the jury, is not about all the evil we know he has done. Our question only deals with Satan's ploy to make the Grace enacted at Calvary with Christ's precious blood of no effect. Is Satan guilty of influencing church doctrine and baptismal practices?

Thank you, members of the jury, for your participation. Before you go to the chamber to deliberate, I stand with my final closing statements. You've heard many witnesses here today. Some of them were not believers, but they still influenced the church. Others were true believers who suffered greatly.

There were many more witnesses I could have called to stand before you. I could have called the Apostles as witnesses. Many of Christ's disciples died the martyr's death, giving their lives defending their God-given Apostolic experience and baptism in Jesus' Name. Eleven of the original twelve disciples were among the martyrs. It is difficult to imagine such a host of witnesses dying for a fabricated falsehood. They lived for the Truth and died for it.

I could have summoned a few Popes who were Bible scholars and independent thinkers—such as Pope Steven I (254-257 AD), Pope Gregory the Great (638 AD), or Pope Nicholas I (858-867 AD). They were men who understood baptism in Jesus' Name as correct even though they held a position of authority in an organization that did not baptize in Jesus' Name. Sadly, they had too short a tenure or too little influence to return organized Christianity to the original Apostolic doctrine.

Instead of calling on Apostles and other church leaders, you heard testimonies of many notable figures from history. You listened to the testimonies of two Roman emperors; both were self-centered and conniving. Each had a sinister hand in the careless treatment of the New Testament church.

You sat and heard the personal account of a man of God who was cast out of the newly engineered Roman Catholic Church because of his refusal to change his belief and baptismal practice.

A lawyer sat on the witness stand and proudly acknowledged his invention of a new word, which fit hand-in-glove with testimonies we heard from two Greek philosophers, neither of whom were Christian.

And we heard the sad account of a physician/statesman/clergyman who died as a martyr during the Reformation, after calling attention to the error of trinitarian doctrine.

You heard accounts from real people who lived. Recorded history bears witness to what happened. It is my hope that you will allow history to speak for itself and impact your understanding of the big picture of religious tradition, political and cultural influence, and the Truth of the Word of God.

Look around at our world today. Satan is still using politics and culture to creep into the church and distort, mislead and corrupt the purity of holiness. Satan is still changing one word at a time, and twisting what God said. Too often the mentality of the church is more like the world than the mind of Christ, but your thoughts don't have to be like the world's outlook. Jesus can transform you by the renewing of your mind. You have the power to decide. What will your response be? Will you stand for Truth?

It is my hope that you will allow history to speak for itself and impact your understanding.

Throughout the court case, I exposed you to a limited array of historic evidence. If what was presented is not enough, there is much more information available. I encourage you to research for yourself. Decide what your verdict will be.

Review the evidence. Read the transcript. Think about the testimony you heard from the witnesses. Check out the references provided. If the argument is compelling, be compelled. The jury is dismissed for deliberation.

As this session of the Court of Eternal Affairs concludes, be prepared. You will be called on again. One day you will stand in the Court of Eternal Affairs before the One Judge, The Spirit of Truth. What will your life's testimony be? What account will you give for your place in time? Have you obeyed God's specific instructions? Your deliberation could rank among the most important thoughts of your life and eternity.

CONCLUSION
A CALL TO ACTION

MY PRAYER FOR YOU is that God's Spirit would light the way to a full understanding of His Truth. I pray you become a strong Soldier of the Cross—through the power of Jesus' Name. I pray your desire to seek Truth intensifies and leads your study and final decisions concerning your eternity. I pray your desire for a relationship with Jesus Christ leads you beyond human relationships and man-made traditions, into the immeasurable heights God designed for you.

In your quest to find, obey and stand for Truth, you need an altar. Maybe it is an altar of repentance. Surely it's an altar of worship. Certainly it will be an altar of communion. We all must commune with God's Spirit—the Spirit of Truth. I pray you will not rest until you begin the pilgrimage to the spiritual places God desires for you.

Many of us have known people who professed to be born again, but still lived out their old natures over and over. They struggled with trying to clean up their language. They fought with lust and immoral lifestyles. They lived a continuous war with their want and desire for possessions and positions. They were not new creations. Old Adam was not dead. He had never been properly buried.

No doubt you have attended the graveside ceremony of some friend or family. What if you returned to the cemetery a few days later only to realize the remains had not been properly buried? You can imagine the result of improper burial.

In the text of this book we spoke clearly of the Gospel of

Christ. We all admit the "death, burial and resurrection" story must be mirrored in our lives to be effective. We

The Apostles and the New Testament believers baptized in "the Name of Jesus." Is there any reason we should do differently today?

know this "death" should follow a distinct dying out to sin through our humble repentance. We hope for the end result of a glorious life full of the "resurrection" power of Jesus! To die properly to sin is only part of the equation. In order to arrive at the proper answer to this life problem, we must team "death" with correct "burial."

Could it be that our problem, for many of us, is that we have repented ever so sincerely, but became sidetracked in our attempt to find a proper burial? Our old sin nature, "Adam," is not buried until he rests in peace under the blood of Jesus. Baptism is the gospel's equivalent for burial. Adam can't truly be buried any other way.

We have illustrated how God's plan and instructions are specific all throughout the Bible. He is still a God of specifics today. In Egypt, at the first Passover, God required sacrifice and the shedding of blood to save His people, but that wasn't all He required. The Israelites had to apply the blood to the doorposts—the door frame—or the death angel would not spare the innocent life of the firstborn.

Today, God requires us to apply the blood of Jesus to our hearts. Jesus bled and died for our sins, and we must apply His blood to our lives to receive remission, or release, from our sins. We must apply that precious blood in His

Name through baptism. Remember, He is the One who shed redeeming blood. As you recall, the devil's trickery changed one word in the baptismal formula—the Name of Jesus—and hijacked the plane of religious teaching concerning baptism. To be more accurate, perhaps Satan merely "misled" or "misinformed" us. He is, after all, the father of lies.

On the day of Pentecost, the people asked the question, *"Men and brethren, what shall we do?"* (Acts 2:37). The Apostle Peter admonished them, *"Repent, and be baptized every one of you in the Name of Jesus Christ for the remission of sins, and ye shall receive the gift of the Holy Ghost"* (Acts 2:38).

The Apostles and the New Testament believers baptized in "the Name of Jesus." Is there any reason we should do differently today?

Just as Mae struggled with her feelings and past experiences, some of us struggle as well. "I can't leave the past," we argue within ourselves. "I can't leave what I always believed to be true. I can't admit that I, and especially those I love who went before me, could have been mistaken, misled or misinformed." We struggle to find the truth. Our thoughts and feelings mix as we wade through the information.

As I try to place myself in your shoes, let me help you put thoughts and feelings into perspective. We are all responsible for what we know. The people who lived before us were responsible for what they knew. You are responsible for what you know now. The Lord sees our hearts, and He is the Judge of our obedience and submission to His Word.

Have you obeyed the Gospel of Jesus Christ—the death, burial, and resurrection? We die in repentance, are buried in baptism in Jesus Name, and are raised to new life by receiving the gift of the Holy Spirit. Are you filled with the Holy Ghost? Only when we properly obey the Gospel of Christ's death, burial and resurrection, can we ever hope to reach our full potential as overcoming, victorious Christians.

Have you been baptized in Jesus' Name? Perhaps you've never been baptized, or maybe you need to be re-baptized the Bible-way. Baptism in the powerful Name of Jesus will bring you one giant step closer to connecting to God's miracle, saving power.

Jesus offers His Grace to work in our lives. He is more powerful than you perhaps ever dreamed. There is power in the blood of Jesus—power to remit, remove and redeem us from sin. Apply His blood to your soul through baptism (Romans 6:3 and 1 John 1:7), calling on His Name (Acts 22:16). Without blood there is no remission of sin (Hebrews 9:22). Animal sacrifice was not enough to redeem us (Hebrews 10:4), but Jesus was the Lamb of God slain from the foundation of the world (John 1:29 and Revelation 13:8). His blood justifies us and saves us (Romans 5:9).

There are churches all over the world that believe and practice baptism as the Apostles did—in Jesus' Name. Some of these churches are called Apostolic, Pentecostal, Oneness, or Jesus' Name. There are many other names, though. Churches of many kinds baptize in Jesus' Name.

As you search for a Bible-believing church, call every church in your area and ask what they believe. Ask, "Do you baptize in the Name of Jesus? Do you believe in the infilling of the Holy Ghost? Do you teach converts to live their lives according to holy Biblical principles?" Don't stop until you find a place of worship that adheres to Biblical Truth, standing against corrupted religious tradition and the ways of the world.

Don't procrastinate. Remember the story of Noah and the ark? God called mankind to get on board. God was in control of the ark's only door. Once it was shut, not even Noah could open it. Don't wait until it's too late. I pray you act now!

John 8:32
*"And ye shall know the truth,
and the truth shall make you free."*

RECOMMENDED READING

A History of Christian Doctrine, by David K. Bernard

A Summary of Christian History, by Robert A. Baker

Ancient Rome, by Simon Baker

Development of the Trinity, by Glen Davidson, MA

Fox's Book of Martyrs, Edited by W.B. Forbush, D.D.

Student's Handbook of Facts in Church History, by Rev. S. C. McClain

When Jesus Became God, by Richard E. Rubenstein

New Advent.org, Catholic Encyclopedia:
The Trinity as a Mystery
The Blessed Trinity
On Baptism
Monarchians

New World Encyclopedia.org:
Sabellius

JIM PICKERING

Jim has lived an interesting and varied life. He worked in industrial mechanics for 44 years and retired as a safety professional in the industry. He also served as EMT for over 30 years.

Beyond work, for the past 50 years his life has revolved around teaching teens and young adults to live their lives as successful Christians. He is a teacher with a drive to communicate important facets of the Christian faith to the world. Along with working with young people, Jim teaches a doctrine class for newcomers at his church.

A native of the Beaumont, Texas area, Jim lives in Vidor, Texas. He and his wife Jewel were married in 1967. They have two sons, Jonathan, and Jody, who is married to Shanna Garris. They have one grandchild, Greyson James, and several "extended family members" and "grandchildren" from their church.

Jim and Jewel attend Eastgate United Pentecostal Church in Vidor, Texas. Jim enjoys gardening, photography, travel and fishing. Jim came to the Lord in 1958, and has lived for God continuously since that time.

You can reach Jim by email at PhotoJim45@gmail.com.

Our Written Lives
book publishing services
www.OurWrittenLives.com